P9-CSA-665

Tommy Catches a Cold

by Sarah Willson

illustrated by Barry Goldberg

SIMON SPOTLIGHT/NICKELODEON

Based on the TV series *Rugrats* created by Klasky/Csupo Inc.
and Paul Germain as seen on Nickelodeon®

SIMON SPOTLIGHT

An imprint of Simon & Schuster Children's Publishing Division
1230 Avenue of the Americas
New York, New York 10020

Manufactured in the United States of America
First Edition   10 9 8 7 6 5
ISBN 0-689-82126-3

On a cold winter day, Tommy and his friends played at the park.

Tommy waddled over to a park bench. He picked up a bottle and took a drink.

Suddenly a shadow fell over him.

"Hey! Thadz *mide!*" said a strange-looking kid with a red nose. Surprised, Tommy handed it to him.

"Hmmm," said Tommy's mother, Didi. "Dr. Lipschitz says that fresh air is good for kids, even in winter. But it looks like there are lots of children here with colds."

"Yep," agreed Betty. "Let's get the kids home before they catch one."

The next morning Tommy woke up feeling strange. His nose didn't work right. His throat tickled.

When Didi saw Tommy she panicked.

"Stu!" she called to Tommy's father. "Tommy is sick!"

"Call an ambulance!" cried Stu, rushing into Tommy's room.

"Ah, pshaw!" said Tommy's grandpa. "The little sprout just caught a bug is all."

"A bug?" Tommy muttered to himself.

"I'll call Dr. Lipschitz," said Didi.

"But it's 5:30 on a Sunday morning!" said Grandpa Lou.

Didi was already racing to the phone. She spoke for a long time, and wrote down a lot of instructions.

Later that morning Stu took Tommy into the bathroom where they stayed for a long time with the shower running. It was hot and steamy.

For the rest of the morning Tommy had to stay on the sofa. Every five minutes Didi felt his forehead and wiped his nose. Then she opened up a big purple jar.

"Just a bit of this spread on your front will help you breathe better," she said. She rubbed the awful-smelling paste on Tommy.

"Hey look, Tommy!" said Stu, coming in from the kitchen. "Your Grandma Minka brought over some old-country chicken soup. Still has the chicken feet in it!"

Later that day Tommy's friends came over. Didi made sure Tommy was placed on the couch, far away from his friends. "Look what I have, Tommy!" said Didi, coming into the room with a big green suction cup.

"This will help unstuff your nose," she assured him.
"Waaaaaaah!" cried Tommy's horrified friends.
Tommy could only whimper.

"I don't thing I can take this anymore!" snuffled Tommy
miserably. "I godda find that bug and led id go!"

"What bug, Tommy?" asked Chuckie.

"The bug I caught ad the playgrowd! It must have got into
the diaper bag, but when I looked id was gone. It's gotta be in
the house somewhere!" said Tommy.

"We'll help you look for it," said Phil.

"Yeah, we'll find it," said Lil.

The babies searched everywhere.
"Is it big, Tommy?" asked Chuckie.
"Prob'ly," said Tommy.
"Should we smoosh it if we find it?" asked Lil.
"No!" said Tommy. "We gotta uncatch it! I mean, we gotta let it go!"

"Now, here's your medicine," said Didi as she returned with a cup. "I mixed in twenty-seven drops of distilled holistic oil of wheat grass into your juice. You won't even taste the medicine."

Luckily for Tommy, the phone rang. "That must be Dr. Lipschitz calling from his European lecture tour!" she said, jumping up.

While she was gone, Tommy slipped the cup of medicine to Chuckie, who hid it behind a plant.

The next day Tommy felt a tiny bit better.

"I don't know," said Didi. "He's still stuffed up. Maybe I should call Lipschitz again."

"Nonsense!" said Grandpa Lou. "In my day we didn't have fancy doctors—just took lots of doses of cod-liver oil. That did the trick."

"Great idea!" said Didi, running for the medicine cabinet.

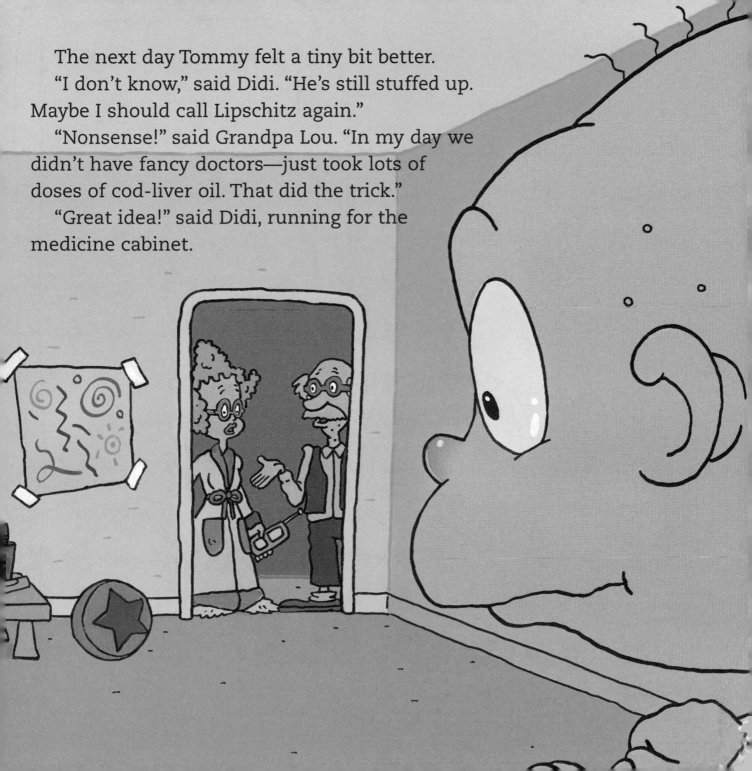

"Keep looking for that bug!" Tommy said to his friends when they came over to visit. "I don't thing I can take any more of thad odd-liver oil."

"Cheer up, Tommy," said Chuckie. "Maybe the bug will fly away by itself."

"Hey, maybe we should open up all the windows and doors," said Phil.

"Maybe we should call the exgerminator," suggested Lil.

Suddenly Tommy's dog Spike growled. He stood stock-still as he stared at something in the corner.

"What is id, ol' boy?" Tommy whispered.

Baying loudly, Spike rushed to the corner and stopped, staring. Tommy and his friends followed. There, behind the plant, was Tommy's abandoned cup of medicine from the day before. And crawling on top of it was a tiny . . . bug.

"I don't like this one bit," said Chuckie fearfully. "That bug could be dangerous."

"Maybe we should call a growed-up," said Lil.

"Nah," said Tommy. "I caught id once, I can catch id again!"

Tommy gently trapped the bug inside his bottle.
Chuckie opened the door. Carefully, gently, Tommy
set the bug free.
"Do you feel any better now?" asked Chuckie.
"Maybe a little," said Tommy.

The next morning Didi went to check up on Tommy.

"Why, Tommy, you look so much better!" she exclaimed. "And here I was coming to bring you a get-well present! It's a mobile with exotic insects from the rain forest." After fastening the mobile to his crib, Didi went to tell Stu the good news.

"Here, boy!" Tommy whispered to Spike, as he removed the mobile. "No more bugs for this baby. But I bet this'll make the perfect chew toy."

Spike stood on his hind legs and barked happily.